Iroda Zokir kizi

WHITE HEART

(Short Stories)

© Iroda Zokir qizi
White Heart *(Short Stories)*
by: Iroda Zokir qizi
Edition: July '2024
Publisher:
Taemeer Publications LLC (Michigan, USA / Hyderabad, India)

© **Iroda Zokir qizi**

Book	:	White Heart *(Short Stories)*
Author	:	Iroda Zokir qizi
Publisher	:	Taemeer Publications
Year	:	'2024
Pages	:	118
Title Design	:	*Taemeer Web Design*

Contents

THE BLACK PRINCE   4
WHITE HEART   16
THRESHOLD   37
SOMEONE   43
BREAD   65
MY EYES ARE ON YOUR HEART   70
THE NINTH SQUARE   76
BEFORE AND AFTER   94

THE BLACK PRINCE

I

I used to think that the whole world was the greenhouse in which I grew up. Now I know that the world does not consist only of sunlight, drops of water, flowers within four walls, and "kind" people in a greenhouse. There are other things in this life. My memories begin in that dark room in my early days when I started growing a vein in a glass jar of water. I was not alone there. There were many flowers like me. Later we were transferred to another place. To be more specific, they planted each of us separately in the soil placed in pots. It was not easy to get used to a new life. But I quickly adapted. After that I was in the greenhouse for a long time. I felt very comfortable there. That's why I grew taller and my leaves got bigger. After some time, they put me and my other partners in dark rectangular boxes and brought them to the flower shop. On the third day of my arrival, a lovely old lady picked me up. Then I came to the old woman's small house in her backpack. The room was very comfortable and well equipped. Rows of pots were lined up along the shelves, and among them were all kinds of flowers. Geranium, aloe, Chinese rose, violet, lavender, hydrangea and even aphelyandra. But I was the only one of my kind. I got to know my roommates. Our old lady took great care of us. Water and food were given in moderation, and there were enough conditions for us to breathe easily. But I was standing in a place where there was too much sunlight. Because of this, my color changed and I became pale. Old lady noticed immediately and moved me over to the lavender on the other shelf. My life was very easy. Our lady to wake up very early in the morning and pray for a long time. Busy with small things during the day, sometimes he would cook in the kitchen, and sometimes he would be busy in the yard. He was eating at the table in the middle of the room until late in the evening. She had a cat named Momiq. She always talked to him while eating and did not forget to treat him with food. Besides Momiq, she sometimes talked to us and stroked our leaves. Sometimes a woman came to our house. I don't know her name, but I didn't like her. Our lady used to talk to her for a long time, and when it got late, she would disappear. One day that woman came again and they talked until the evening, the woman left, and the mistress thought for a long time in the dark room without even turning on the light. Then he came to the shelf and grabbed my wide spread leaves.

– My black prince, – she said while stroking my leaves, – You are the prince of all the flowers here, as well as the protector. Keep your waist straight and your leaves wide. I trust you. Be a support to other flowers as my son is a support to me. My son is abroad now. He works there and lives with my sweet grandson and my daughter-in-law in a house four times larger than this one. I haven't seen my grandson yet. But I imagine he with the image of my son when he was a child. Although my son is far from me, I live on him. If I die, he is my only supporter who will shake my grave and bury me. You see, he will definitely come. Brings my daughter-in-law and grandson. Then we will live in this house as a family. The house is a bit small, but that's okay with us. They say that there is less interest in big houses. Okay, I will give my room to my son and daughter-in-law. I go to the kitchen. It is also a warm, comfortable place. It was enough for my son to come. My daughter mistakenly thought that he would not come. He will definitely come, you'll see!

Then she spoke to the rest of the flowers one by one. Although there was pain in her words, her tongue seemed to caress for some reason, which encouraged us. It started to rain outside. Mistress took us out into the yard and left us in the rain. I was very happy about it. Which flower doesn't like the rain? Is there anything in this world that is more enjoyable than standing under a drop of rain and basking in the soothing music of the rain ?!

II

Over the next few days, the lady became ill. She laid on the bed by the window with her eyes fixed on the outside all day, and her daughter was here every day. Beka didn't even taste salt all day, and when she heard a knock, she would knock on the door. She was waiting for her son and prayed to God for her safe return. But a week later, there was no sign of her son. She was talking to us lying in bed, telling us that she saw her son in a dream. At that moment, I began to want that boy to return. If he came, the mistress would be cured and we would return to our previous leisurely days.

The next day, we, that is, all the flowers, were transferred to the dining room. This was done by the mistress's daughter. Ten minutes later the flowers that had just been neatly picked on the windowsill were lying haphazardly in the corner of the kitchen. This place was very uncomfortable for us. There was no sunlight at all. The air was also stuffy. We stayed here for another week. I was short of breath, and I hadn't even drunk water in a long time. Mistress's daughter came in and out of the kitchen every day and did not pay attention to us. Mistress was not seen at all. On the day they were moved here, the mistress's low, broken voice could be heard from the other room. But for a week now, this voice has not been heard. I thought that maybe when the son came, he took the mistress away. However, I did not see a single stranger in the room.

The soil was drying up more and more, and I felt restlessness in my body. My straight inch began to bend. I called our mistress, but no one could hear me. The condition of the other flowers could not be said to be good either. During the day I just dozed off and did not notice anything. One day, I was dozing as usual when I woke up with a jolt. I saw that the mistress's daughter was loading the flower baskets one by one into a cart. Then I fell asleep again. When I opened my eyes, I found myself back at the counter. It was the same flower shop where my lady bought me.

III

I stayed at the flower shop for ten days. On the eleventh day of my arrival, the shop owner gave me as a gift to a little girl. To be more precise, the girl helped the owner of our flowershop to bring her bag of flowers to the store. The lady gratefully told the little girl, who was looking at the flowers on the counter with interest and wonder, that she could choose from the last flowers on the counter. I was the choice of the little girl, who was thinking for a long time about which flower to choose. After that, I went to her house with the little girl in my arms. The girl took me into the living room and greeted the man sitting on the armchair. This man must have been the girl's father. The little girl turned to her father, who was holding me in his arms. I think she was waiting for her father to ask her where she got the flower from, and to hear a word of praise from him telling her about good work today. But the father, who was sitting with a cigarette, did not say anything to her. The girl left me on the table and went inside. The room was cramped and messy. The clothes on the shelf were strewn about, and the floor was covered with shards of broken glass. After a while, the man walked up to the phone with a half–smoked cigarette in one hand. He hesitated for a long time and started dialing a number. A woman's voice came from the other side.

"...Hello... Please don't hang up. Please forgive me. This will not happen again. I promise you...not a lie. I'm telling the truth...I promise I'll stop drinking...For our children, please..."

Two hours later, a young child was heard crying in the other room. It was joined by noisy voices. It seemed that the landlady had returned. The man came to him with a happy face. For the next hour, the woman's cries did not stop. And I began to dream.

In the morning I opened my eyes shivering from the cold air. The windows of the room were left open, and the woman was tidiing the house with frustration. Either because she was too busy with work or because she was like that, she didn't even look back at me. While wiping the table, he put me on the window sill and continued her work. I spent the day in such a dull mood.

IV

Thirteen days. It's been so many days since I came home. There were no events of note during this time period. I'm still on that shelf. I think I'm the only house flower in this house. No other flower was visible. Lady was angry. During the day, she would spend time with his children. They had three children. She used to beat her son a lot because he made a lot of trouble. During the day, only the child's crying and the angry mother's screams did not stop. Such an environment began to squeeze me from all four sides.

One day in the middle of the night I woke up from shouting. Around it was dark. The door of the bedroom was falling open from the crack, and the shouting voices were coming from there. Suddenly the door opened with a bang and the man came out. He staggered over and threw himself into a chair. Woman was still chattering, and the man was smoking a cigarette, not paying attention to what she was saying. Despite his promises, he was still drinking today. This is probably the reason for the quarrel. The acrid smoke of smoking tobacco surrounded the whole room like fog. I was out of breath. I couldn't breathe. At that moment, I wanted the mistress to open the window and ventilate the room, but I knew that the mistress, who was still cursing, would not think of it. She ventilates the room only in the morning. But at the same time, there will be more fights in the morning than now. On the one hand, if I look forward to the dawn, on the other hand, if it doesn't dawn, I would say...

When I woke up the next day, I found myself in the children's room. I was so glad that now I was free from the shouting in the hotel. Besides, I could be with the little girl day and night, watching over her. The little girl noticed that I was turning yellow in the tub, and apparently she poured water on my roots, removed dust from my leaves. Although the children's room is very small, at least there is no bitter and smelly tobacco smoke, and I could breathe easily. I started to feel better as water ran through my veins. But my dark leaves turned pale. The little girl (I don't know her exact age, but she was small) didn't go out much with her older brother. Taking care of her little brother was his main duty. Her mother is busy with housework during the day, relationship with her husband is still the same, she used to quarrel with him in the evening when he was drunk. At such times, the little girl who woke up from the noise would get up, close the door tightly, lean on the shelf and watch the outside. Sometimes I would see her crying with her ears covered. At such times, I felt sorry for the little girl. I wanted to caress and comfort him, but it hurt that I was powerless in this regard.

V

One month. It's been a month since I came to this apartment. I want to see my old lady. I miss her house, the times I spent there with flowers. My condition is getting worse and worse. My leaves have dried up and fallen off. I have only three leaves left. I am not a "black prince", but a sickly blue flower. I still care about the little girl, but she is still small. Not old enough to take care of me. I want to stand in the rain and bask in the fresh, humid air. I doze off all day long. My body is sinking more and more to the ground.

VI

Last night I woke up from the voice of a little girl. He rested his chin on the shelf, looked up at the sky, and prayed to God that his parents would not fight. I was crushed inside. I wish I had a human voice and could shout as loud as I could, the insults heard from the next room would stop for a moment and they would hear me... If I could comfort the little girl's heart that needs love. I stroked her head and said hello... The girl put her head on the shelf and fell asleep. She couldn't hear me.

At that moment the door opened and the mistress entered. She woke up his sleeping son by pushing him. Surprised that the girl was sleeping in such a state, she stared at her for a while and shook her awake. Although the sleepy children did not understand what was happening, the mistress began to dress them.

"You're not going anywhere!" – the owner's voice came from the corridor.

"Get out of the way, I'll go anyway." Even when I leave, I will not return! – said woman, – all you need is alcohol. Nothing else is needed. Even if you don't think about me, you should think about your children.

"Stop it!" – the man got angry, threw the bed sheets over, and started to break the things on the shelf one by one.

I closed my eyes. But he didn't ignore me either. He grabbed it with both hands and threw it towards his wife. As I hit the wall, I heard the little girl say "No". But whether he said it because I could touch his penis or because he felt sorry for me, it was unclear to me. All I remember is: a strong blow, my body breaking into pieces, broken bones scattered everywhere, and my last breath... Then the sky appeared. The sky was full of white clouds, but it was raining. The little girl was brushing my leaves in the rain, and I was talking with her...

WHITE HEART

"He's gone," I felt as if my body was filled with anguish. As I clutched the photo in my hand, I saw his wrinkled face. Why did he leave without telling me... various thoughts were buzzing in my head, in front of me was 8-year-old Javlon, who was being caressed in his father's arms, and his "wrinkled uncle" who hugged him tightly with his rough fingers came... Only then did I realize that this news should be greeted with joy...

It all started with convicts serving their sentences coming to work at the furniture store located at the beginning of our street. When I first heard this news from my friend Makhmud, I was shocked. When I heard the word "prisoner", I saw in my mind the scary faces with beards and mustaches that I saw in the movies. When the rest of my friends thought the same as me, we left our way to and from the furniture store and went around the other side of the street. I was not afraid of anything when I went to school because my friends were with me. However, the most frightening thing of all was going to the drawing club. The art school was on the east side of street and to get there you had to pass by the furniture store. It was a very difficult situation for small-hearted children like me. I went with my brother for a couple of days at the beginning because I was going to art school at the same time as my brother was going to school. When we passed by the furniture store, I would take a couple of fearful glances in the direction of the store. At such a time, hardly anyone was seen in the workshop yard, only the rhythmic whirring of the machines and the noisy sounds of people could be heard. From the third day, the time of our club changed, and now I had to go to training alone. I set off with my big folder of white papers in my hand. For some reason, my walking steps seemed to slow down when I came to the furniture store. I looked in the direction of the workshop yard. No one was visible in the yard, the machines were working as usual. My fear seems to have subsided a bit and I passed the "danger zone" "safely". It was a victory for me. That's probably why my drawings in class turned out to be very similar, for which I received a special praise from my teacher. I started the lesson again in a happy mood (the lesson ended in the evening because the time was delayed). By the time I got to the "danger zone" my steps were as slow as ever. There were a lot of people standing in the yard, in the dark it was impossible to tell which of them were ordinary workers and which were "hired" workers. The most disturbing thing was that one of them was leaning on the wire wall with his hands and looking towards the street at me. I don't remember what I was thinking at that moment. As far as I know, I'm running as fast as I can. After passing through the "danger zone", I looked back and the man was still looking at me. I ran again.

The next day, in order to go to training, I went to their place with my friend Makhmud's bicycle. He was sitting on his bed in the middle of the yard looking at his toys. "The bicycle is near the gate." he said. I told him that I would bring the bike to him in the evening.

– Do your classes end so late? – he wondered, – aren't you afraid?

– No, – I said hesitantly.

– My sister has a classmate, Ma'ruf, who lives at the end of the street, do you know her?

– Yes, I know. What is not?

– That night, when he was returning from his uncle's house, a man came out of the yard of the furniture store and chased him. The poor man ran as hard as he could and barely escaped. The next day, he couldn't even go to school because he had a cold.

I was so scared that I gasped.

– Now, be careful just in case.

After I dragged the bike home, I forgot about the incident. Because I was interested in riding a bicycle, I probably didn't care about my surroundings and made it to the art school. This time our teacher taught us how to draw a portrait. The exercise was quite difficult. It was too late before I finished. I started to ride my bike on the dark road. As I passed by the furniture store, I started thinking about as many good things as possible to distract myself. The darkness was very thick. Suddenly, the bicycle balloon hit something and crashed. I lost my balance and fell on my side. My whole body trembled from the strong blow. There was no one on the street. At that moment, some kind of ghost came out of the yard of the furniture store. Footsteps were coming closer and closer, and I thought someone was coming towards me. Suddenly, I remembered what Makhmud had told me, and panic filled my heart. I was scared and didn't know what to do. I wanted to scream, but my voice wouldn't come out. My legs were stuck under the bike, and it was impossible to escape. Tears fell from my eyes, whether it was from pain or fear, I was not in a position to analyze. In the meantime, another person came to me. I closed my eyes and put my head between my shoulders, thinking that he is going to kill me now. One, two... An unknown person arrived and took away the bicycle that had stepped on my feet.

– Can you get up?

Only then did I open my eyes. He took my arm and stood me up, patting my dusty pant legs.

– Your knee is just a little sprained. This is the situation that many people like you are in. Where is your house? Whose son are you?

– At the end of the street, – I stammered.

– Can you walk by yourself?

I hastily nodded. At that moment, a bicycle came to my mind.

– My bike!

– Here is your bicycle. The steering wheel tilted. Not suitable for driving. Take the lead.

Tears came out of my eyes. When I took it to Makhmud, I said that I would return it the way it was. What happens now?

– Why are you crying, or does your wound hurt?

– The bike was not mine, how can I return it to the owner,– I said.

– This may cause a quarrel, – uncle shook his head, – if you want, leave him. I'll fix it by tomorrow morning. If the owner asks, say I will take it out tomorrow, ok?

There was no other option at that time. As soon as I take the bike, there is no one to fix it. My brother can't. My father went on a trip.

– Okay.

When I came home, I thought a lot about the unknown uncle. It was obvious that he was a prisoner from the clothes he was wearing. I was very surprised by his kindness. From what I heard from my comrades and in my imagination, the "prisoner" was a stone-faced, merciless criminal. I thought they didn't have emotions like normal people. It seemed that no good could be expected from lawbreakers. However, today's work and the help of a stranger uncle caused me to hesitate from my previous thoughts, a battle of thoughts was beginning in my heart...

The next morning, as usual, my mother ordered me to bring milk to our neighbor Sabokhat aunty two houses away. The aunt's only son came to see her daughter, who had moved abroad with her family and became a bride in the neighboring district, once a month . Hugging a warm jar of freshly expressed milk, I set off. Sabohat, as always, prayed and emptied the jar. I left my aunt's house and went straight to the furniture store. I stopped at the door of the workshop. On the other side of the yard, where no one could see, a woman was sweeping the yard with frustration. The woman saw me staring and walked towards me. I greeted when I approached. He asked who I was waiting for. Only then did I remember that I had not asked the name of the unknown uncle.

– I don't know his name. I left my bike yesterday. He said he would fix it by morning.

– Does he work here? – Aren't you talking about the old guard?

– No, he was not an old man. He...– for some reason I didn't want to say "prisoner".

– There are many workers here. Moreover, the working hours have not yet started. The workers' bedroom is in the inner building. They won't let you in. Militias stand. Better yet, come another time.

I was desperately turning back when someone called "hey" behind me. I turned around and saw that unknown uncle with a bicycle in his hand. I ran to him.

He put the bicycle handlebars in my hands.

– Now take this to the owner immediately. Don't make another mistake.

– Thank you, uncle.

I raised my head and looked at his face. It's funny that I didn't see his face well because it was dark last night. His uncle's dark, rough face, with two large wrinkles on his forehead, seemed to glisten in the sun.

– What is your name? – he said staring at my face.

– My name is Javlon.

Uncle was silent. He seemed at a loss for what he wanted to say.

– My son's name is Javlon too. He is 8 years old. How old are you?

– I'm 12.

I quickly said goodbye saying that I will be late for school.

That's how we got to know wrinked uncl. For some reason, when I think of him, the first thing that comes to my mind is the wrinkles on his forehead, that's why I named him "wrinkled uncle". Every day, if not every day, I would see him in the yard of the shop. He called my name from afar and waved merrily. I waved to him gratefully, now this place no longer seemed like a "dangerous area" to me, I was no longer afraid. One day, I was returning early from training, and I noticed a wrinkled uncle sitting by the wire fence, thinking. For some reason, I wanted to talk to him at least a little. I went and greeted him. It seems that he was startled as he sat in thought. He was on the inside of the wire fence and I was on the outside.

– Didn't I scare you?

– No, I'm just thinking. Are you coming home from class?

– It is possible to say so. After scholl, I attend drawing class.

– I know,– he said with a smile.

– How know about it? I didn't tell yet?"

– I watch you a lot. You go to school with your friends in the morning. In the afternoon, you carry your big folder and go wherever you go. Only artists or architects have this folder.

– Yes, you are right.

– Can you show me your drawings.

I opened my folder and showed my works, some unfinished, some finished. He watched for a long time with pleasure.

– You draw beautifully. You have the feat to do this, – he said.

Among my drawings, two images of pigeons flying in the blue sky caught his attention.

– Pigeons, – he whispered softly.

– Yes, a pigeon, – I claimed.

Then he remembered that his son loved birds and had a pair of canaries at home.

At that moment, a car stopped near the gate. Two women, one of whom was probably an old woman, were walking, and a man came down. All three had luggage in their hands.

– Who are they? Do you know?

– My partner's family members. They came to see.

– Will your family come too?

– Yes, of course.

– What about your son?

– My son...he won't come, or rather I told him not to come.

– Why? – I said without hiding my surprise.

– I just don't want him to see me like this.

– What happened to you?

– Kid, you don't understand these things yet.

– May I ask you a question?"

– Well?

– How did you get here?

His eyes were fixed on me and he was silent. I don't know what he felt at that moment. It was dark to me, but I couldn't bear to look into his sad eyes. I looked away. I'm sorry for asking such a rude question.

– If it's difficult to answer, you don't have to.

– No, – he said, – It's not difficult to answer. I will answer your question later, ok?

We did not talk long. We said a cold goodbye. He appointed me to bring milk tomorrow.

I didn't tell my mom that I made friends with my wrinkled uncle. I was afraid that if he found out, he would ban me from seeing him. My mother was a bit more nervous by nature. Therefore, I was thinking about how I will take milk to my wrinkled uncle tomorrow. If I told the truth, it was only natural that my mother would ask how I met her. And then there was the fact that he ordered me not to go near a blind, dangerous person, and he forbade me to meet him. After thinking about it, I found a solution. Aunt Sabo doesn't say anything if I don't take her one day, and the next day I come up with an excuse. My uncle took the milk and put money in my hand as he returned the empty can.

– This is for milk. You give it to the moon.

– I can't take the money, – I said.

– Why?

I didn't know what to say. But I didn't want to take money from him either. I said the first thing that came to my mind.

– My mother said don't take money. She get upset if I don't do what she say.

Uncle smiles.

– Then thank your mom on my behalf.

– Okay.

– By the way, can you bring milk tomorrow?

– Okay, but you never had milk before."

– I've got a cold. People say that milk is good for cough.

– My mom also give a lot of milk when my throat hurts and I start to cough.

– Your mother is right.

I hugged the empty jar and went home. I hated myself for lying first to my mother and then to my uncle. However, I had no choice. For a week, I took the milk my mother gave for aunt Sabokhat to her wrinkled uncle.

Days passed. In the meantime, my friends found out about my relationship with my wrinkled uncle. Makhmud started making all kinds of comments to me. If I walk with them, they say, "Don't walk with us. "There is a friend you met on the street," they would say, walking away from me as if I were in the company of a serious criminal. I am disappointed with them. After all, it is not a sin to make friends, why everyone calls the wrinkled uncle and others like him criminals. I couldn't find answers to the questions that filled my heart. I don't know what crime the wrinkled uncle did. But I can say for sure that he deeply regrets it.

One day, when I was returning from school as usual, I saw my uncle sitting on a chair behind a wire wall. It's been more than a week since we talked. I went to him. He was staring at some kind of paper, tears welling up in his eyes. He looked up at the sound of footsteps. As always, he was on one side of the wire fence, and I was on the other side (for some reason, he never invited me inside).

– I received a letter from my son, he said, showing the paper in his hand, – he wrote that he is studying with good grades. He said that he will learn to play chess before you come.

– What about you, do you know?

– Yes, I have a lot of achievements in it, you know that too?

– Yes, but I'm not strong.

Uncle smiles:

– You're still getting stronger. My son didn't know either. He is attending a club. I wonder why I didn't teach him chess myself when I was at home?!

He dug into his bosom and pulled out a rough, frayed picture.

– This is my son Javlon.

He passed the picture to me through the wires of the wall. In the picture, a 5–6–year–old boy with dark eyebrows and curly hair was smiling.

– He's not like you.

– Yes, – he agreed.

I saw my comrades on the other side of the street. When they saw me, they began to whisper. Makhmud pointed to me with folded hands and said something. Uncle noticed that I was staring at them.

– Your friends?

–Yes.

– Then stay with them.

– No, – I said, shaking my head.

– Why?

- I hate them! – I expressed my hatred in these words.
- Why do you hate them? Did you fight?

I told you everything. Uncle laughed.

– They are not guilty. Don't be upset with them. Just because they think like that, you and I are not bad. You explain to them. Once he lost his way, it doesn't mean that he will stay on it forever. It's true, not everyone is brought here, there is one mistake, that's what happened. However, no one wants to stay away from his family in such a difficult situation. I can't tell you what I saw and felt here, but what hurts the most is the pain I felt when I looked into the eyes of my wife and son, who were waiting for me. You do not understand these things, my God, never let it happen to you. Javlon, my son, you should study very well, become a great artist, depict wide horizons, endless fields, beautiful places in your paintings. May people see your pictures and be thankful that they live in such a life, appreciate freedom and... and... – he looked at his colleagues working inside – may those who lost the liferoad find the right path!

He was called, he hurriedly said goodbye and went inside. I stood still clutching the picture in my hand. The image of Javlon stuck with me. I put it in my folder for the next time we meet.

When I came home, I started thinking about Javlon for some reason. I saw an 8-year-old boy leaning over the table and writing a letter to his father. I took a pencil in my hand and started to write down his face in the picture. I am very busy with work. I finished Javlon's portrait after dark. For some reason, I drew him with a happier face than in the picture. Then suddenly I thought that I should draw his wrinkled uncle next to him. It was a good idea, but since I didn't have a picture of my uncle, I had to draw it in my mind. It was very complicated. But, I started trying hard. On the third day, I was satisfied with the painting. The picture shows Javlon, whose eyes are shining with joy, and his wrinkled uncle, who is smiling next to him. I didn't draw the wrinkles on his uncle's forehead, for some reason I didn't want to draw them.

I wanted to take the photo the next day as soon as I got home from school. When I came home from school in a happy mood, my mother and aunt Sabohat were talking near our gate. I said hello and passed. For some reason, my mother reacted coldly. Dad is at home too. I had just finished changing my clothes when my mother entered the door. I was scared when I saw my mother's expression. "Aunt Sabohat told my mother that I haven't taken milk for a week" flashed in my mind and this thought came to me.

– What are you doing?

My father looked at me and at my month.

– What happened, dear?

– Don't worry. I didn't know what this kid was up to. For a week now, Sabo has been taking the milk he gave to his mother to the prisoner. His comrades also confirmed. For a month, he has been hanging around the furniture store. The two of them talked for hours in the sex yard. Oh, sorry. What do you have to do with a prisoner? What is left in it that you see every day!

I was wondering what to say. My mother was constantly babbling, and my father was staring at me with a furrowed brow.

— A criminal is a criminal by name. They are not good people. You have to go beyond them. What would we do if they kidnapped you or force to be drugged you?!

No, I couldn't stand these words anymore. A voice was shouting inside me, I couldn't say anything outside. Why should I be silent, I said to myself. I don't know if I'm guilty, if I keep quiet, after all, the wrinkled uncle is a good person. He never invited me to do bad things.

"It's not as you think, honey!" my voice echoed around the room. My mother stopped talking for a while and became silent, – why do you think they are bad, it does not mean that one mistake does not mean that you will stay on this path for the rest of your life. They are very nice people. Uncle also deeply regrets what he did. He will never stray from his path. He never invited me to do bad work. Why do you call them bad, after all, they are human beings too. They should also return to their lives, they will not remain in this brand forever!

Tears filled my eyes. But I didn't cry. I hugged the picture in my hand and left the house. I went straight to the furniture store. I asked the guard to call his wrinkled uncle." They pardoned him. He went home this morning."

It was as if my body was covered with some kind of agony. As I clutched the photo in my hand, I saw his wrinkled face. Why did he leave without telling me, ... various thoughts were buzzing in my head, in front of me was 8–year–old Javlon, who was being caressed in his father's arms, and his "wrinkled uncle" who hugged him tightly with rough fingers came... Only then did I realize that I should welcome this news with joy.

THRESHOLD

A door with faded blue paint. A gloomy threshold. Two pairs of shoes. This is the view dog see under a new mulberry branch that has just grown on the edge of the yard, just opposite the threshold. The dog hasn't been brought in for long, so it quietly observes the surroundings with a slightly alienated bark. As it lay there, it could see the scene: a door with faded blue paint, two pairs of shoes. One of the shoes is large, with a padded sole, and the second is much smaller and thinner than the first. Usually, there is only one pair of shoes on the doorstep during the day, and one more pairs appear at night. Since the dog is still new, it does not know the owners of the shoes well. Therefore, they can only be distinguished from shoes. There are few people visible in the yard. Here, for some reason, the shouting that can be heard from the neighboring yards is replaced by silence. When the dog hears the screams of the children coming from the neighboring house, it jumps up and spins around with its tail wagging. The dog looks around, looking for the source of the noise, and when he doesn't find it, he goes back to his place. It spends the day barking at strangers at the front door and lying on the doorstep. In the evening, a pair of shoes on the doorstep is always joined by a second pair. The clinking of cups and spoons can be heard from the dimly lit room. The dog sticks out his tongue and licks his tail. Because every time after such voices they bring it food. After the dog is full, it goes back to its place on the threshold. A quiet night falls. The stars begin to shine like embers in the clear sky. It pulls at the chain, trying to loosen it, even though he knows it's ineffective. But the chain does not move. Finally, the dog surrenders to its fate and lies listening to the barking of dogs in the distance, and sometimes he joins them. The outside world seems more interesting to him than the quiet world in which he lives. This is probably why he dreams of breaking its chains and traveling to the world he is interested in.

Night is replaced by morning, and morning is replaced by night. The river flows forward, and the sun rises. Two pairs of shoes continue to stand on the threshold, sometimes together, sometimes alone. The dog also gets used to this flat, uneventful quiet life, and now he himself becomes a part of this silence. The yard is still the same, but the mulberry branch is now a larger tree. Previously, the dog could barely fit in its shadow, but now it can comfortably lie down with its legs stretched out. Some days, another pair is added to the shoes on the doorstep. The dog does not like the owner of these shoes. This woman, who comes here every now and then, starts a commotion every time she comes. On the day of her arrival, shoes standing on the threshold are also removed under the sole. The wife treats everyone around the table. Her rude words make the dog angry. At first it growls, then it begins to bark with pain. The dog, with its own sensitivity, notices that after the wife leaves, the mistress cries, and the master becomes distraught.

Night and morning do not stop changing places, a belligerent wife comes and leaves to upset the mistress. The shadow of the mulberry is now enough to cover not only the dog, but also its surroundings.

One day, the dog wakes up in the middle of the day. They stretch their legs forward. When it looked up, dog saw that there were four pairs of shoes standing on the threshold, not two, as usual. He is very interested in stranger shoes. He wants to go and smell it. Its constant trick: it starts trying to break the wire chain by biting it. After trying hard for a long time, it finally succeeds. The wire rope is loose and the chain tied to the stake and falls to the ground. The dog runs around the yard to write its paws. Touching something, it silently walks towards the threshold, so as not to let the mistress know that he is free.

Here are "strangers" next to the usual two pairs of shoes. One is as big as a master's, and the other is very similar to a mistress's delicate shoes. As the dog approaches them to sniff them, it suddenly stops. In the middle of the "strangers" stands another shoe, which is very, very small compared to them. The dog has never seen anything like this before, so he begins to observe the little frog with surprise and interest. A pair of well–crafted shoes, decorated with colorful glitters, will be very pleasing to her. The dog bends down and sniffs. There is a pleasant smell that you have never encountered before. It carefully bites a leg of a thorn in its mouth and brings it to the mulberry shade. The dog that did not go near the mulberry when it was loosed from the chain for fear of being tied again, now stretches out in the shade of the mulberry tree without even thinking about it. While looking at this mysterious little shoe standing in front of him, he sniffs it once more. The dog, that usually gets mad when a shoe falls on its hand, is not in a hurry now for some reason. With its forepaws, it flips over the fat of the tiny baby. Footsteps are heard from the house. The dog raises its head and looks in the direction of the sound and licks its tail when it sees its mistress coming towards it. Mistress stops, her eyes falling on the shoe on the dog's lap. She tries to reach out, but the dog resists by growling. Woman's hand hangs in the air. Looking at a dog and a pair of shoes between its front legs, it seems to become clear to him what the dog wants.

– Olapar, – she says in a trembling voice.

The dog looks up when it hears own name.

– Did you like it? I like it too. You know, these shoes are perfect for our threshold.

A woman stares at the shelter in the corner of the yard. Two drops of tears rolled down from his eyes and fell on the dog's feet. The dog is petted.

– If you knew, I would exchange the whole world for this pair of shoes... – she thought for a moment, and suddenly stood up and wiped her tears.

– Olapar, that's it. Go ahead. – the mistress hurriedly takes a pair of shoes and turns back.

The dog stubbornly runs after the mistress. When he reaches the threshold, he meets a boy who is slightly taller than him and has a chubby face. The boy was frightened by the dog and hid behind the porch post. Mistress drags the dog to the place and ties it up so that the boy will not be afraid. The dog lies staring at the strange boy. For some reason, it doesn't bother him...

As evening falls, the guests leave, and the courtyard is again silent. A weary night falls. This is how the days go by. Morning and night alternate, the sun rises and sets. The shade of an old mulberry now comfortably covers almost half of the yard. The dog spends the day only dozing. While awake, it looks around indifferently from between its drooping eyelids. The scene before him is still the same: a double-glazed door, a tarnished threshold, two pairs of shoes...

SOMEONE

Worthless are looking for value,

The dead are alive without a grave.

The living are impatient.

My soul cannot live in a body.

(Shakhrizod Shodiyev)

It is difficult to wake up in the morning. Whether it is because I slept late or because I was very tired, I don't want to get up even when the alarm clock rang for the third time. But I have to go to work. Helplessly, I get up. Yesterday, it "increased" a bit, and I had a buzzing pain as if a swarm of bees had entered into my head. After washing in the cold water, I regain consciousness. I'm used to the fact that such "buzzing" happens occasionally, if not every day. After a cold shower and two cups of hot coffee, I feel like a relaxing. I go to the kitchen. I begin to wait for the water to boil while watching the surroundings from the window. As the sun rises, the weather seems cold, people on the street are wearing jackets, jackets, and similar warm clothes. As soon as I open the window, the cold but pleasant air came in. I took a deep breath. The smell of roasting corn wafted from the cucumber stand far away, mixed with the pungent smell of rain. I start chilling, but my body likes it. The kettle whistles. It is only when I open the cupboard to make coffee that I remember that I had brewed the last coffee in the box yesterday. "Damn it! Now you have to go down. I am in a hurry to work. But I can't do without coffee." Reluctantly, I hang my cloak over me and go out.

"Even when Bakhora was at home, she would bring me. I wouldn't walk on the street with my slippers on at such a time. That's what a woman is: she can't be found anywhere. I can live without her, but she still regrets a lot. A woman's fate is good or bad. Should he get used to theher spouse?"

Five minutes passed before I got a box of coffee out of the store. When I get home and put the key in the door, I see an envelope lying under the floor. I wonder if there is envelope when I left my home? Or do they pass while I am in the store? But I paid for a box of coffee and left.

At first I think the letter is a reminder to pay utility bills. But when I get home, I open the envelope. The envelope is not addressed. When I open it to my surprise, I find a letter. Slightly right–skewed but legible writing filled half of the white paper.

Hello, dear!

Have you kick out your wife home and live like a free bird? So, are those rascals who are dearer and more valuable than your wife, serving you with all their heart? Or burning in the fire of regret, eating your head with a thousand different thoughts?

Don't try hard...you can't get rid of these thoughts in this world. They come to your mind every day, and they continue to carve your brain like a needle. Be careful, your brain is your only working organ...

Be safe. Don't bother trying to find out who wrote the letter. You won't find me. But if you want, I will leave you right away. Wishing you honesty and patience

Love Someone

It's so weird... I start to think which of my acquaintances could come up with such a ridiculous joke. No one come to my mind except my classmate Rustam. It has been. That's exactly it. Previously, he used to write unknown messages from various unknown numbers and make jokes. Although this custom still exists . Now it has gone to an unknown letter. An unsolved slave! That's the kind of acting that's necessary. On the one hand, I laughed, and on the other hand, I was angry with my friend, who is "worrying" so much without resorting to petty gossip. After leaving work, I decided to go into his office, drank my coffee and ran to the office. Because the end of the month is near, there is a lot of work to bury a person, it is time to scratch the head and blink the eyelashes. "Work, work, only work" You can't turn around and talk to your colleague. It is possible to breathe freely only during sleep. It will not take more than an hour. With that, until the evening, more papers full of numbers are waiting for us. Only the "sing–sing" of the computer keys and the rumbling sounds coming from the reception area can be heard throughout the room . In the accounting department, the peacekeeper, as his name suggests, only eats eyes and hands. If your tongue gets in the way, a small mistake will be born, and it will lead to the birth of others similar to it.

There is nothing worse than that. At five–thirty, the other employees disappear one by one. But our department often stays open until dark.

I leave work around seven o'clock. It is very cold. The sky is covered with a curtain of dark clouds, and he looks sad and sad like a patient lying on his death bed . A flesh–chilling October wind is blowing around. I started walking. The pocket cannot afford to take a taxi . In addition, he has to endure the drag of friends, who "visit" every weekend, to various restaurants and places of rest. My phone rang. As soon as I read the name "Rustam" on the screen, I remember the unknown letter from the morning. I smile and pick up the phone. Rustam's voice, instead of sounding cheerful as I expect, sounded serious and quiet. From Rustam's phone calls I know, that he needs money. Things are not the same. He is in debt. He should earn money in three days. I couldn't afford to pay him. I explain the situation correctly . Rustam pretend to be offended and said goodbye. I stop him and ask if he come to my home today. He has been living in his village for a week. He had to hire a tenant for his house in the city. I quickly said goodbye to Rustam.

Although I sleep late in the evening, for some reason I was sleepy and wake up early in the morning. I am thinking while waiting for alarm clock. Another day begin, no different from any other. The same life, consisting only of home and work, sometimes bores a person. As if you are the only one left in this world. He says that he will be swallowed up by the whirlwind of the city. You are one side, and your desires are the other side. During my mother's life, I often went to the village. After my mother 's death, I rarely went there. I was doing whatever I could. Am I staring at my brother?! As soon as he sees me in front of him, he opens his bag of advice. What are you saying: Reconciliation with Bakhora. I should fear God. What have I done to fear God? I was not happy with Bakhora since we start new life together. How to be happy after five years?! Moreover, God did not give any children. After that, what should I do?! Besides, she doesn't love me. I married her to quarrel with her?!

Bakhora thinks as I am a sinner in front of the her. This is the reason why God did not give children. If I want to have children, I need to straighten my gait. When I ask what happened to me, she says, "Do you think I don't know anything?"

"What if you know?" What could you do?! If you know that I will betray you, then why are you standing here, leave! – I said.

I don't know what the will of a woman is, I thought she would leave right away. But she still stared at me without saying a word, "Fear God!" and went out to the kitchen. I went to work with that. I came back in the middle of the night. To be honest, I thought she had already gone to her mother. That's why we sat and drank with Rustam. When I come, she is still at home. She is waiting for me in the middle of the night without sleeping. I'm sick. When I was little, if my brother and I got into a fight, my mother would beat me. I was angry with my mother, and I planned that I would not speak to my mother for a week and regret that she had beaten me. After an hour, my mother would come and talk to me. I felt humiliated. Why am I a dog that first beats and then immediately caresses?! This act of Bakhora reminded me of that. I was tired and went to the hotel. I stopped talking to her at all. We lived alone for two months. She tried a lot to talk to me, to reconcile, but I didn't bother. I openly betrayed him. I was talking on the phone in front of my eyes. I came home when I wanted, I left when I wanted. I worked like "Let's see how far your patience will go". My goal was to break up with her completely. And finally, one day I achieved this intention. Come home late as always, and when I come back drunk, Bakhora is waiting for me again. I was walking to the hotel without saying a word, he stopped me. She began to cry. Then she asked how long this situation will continue and told him to live like people. I told I wanted to break up with her. "I will marry someone else who will give birth to a child for me. If you have pride, how can you stand to live in such humiliation, the sooner you leave this house, the better!" I said and went into my room. When I wake up in the morning, the house is quiet. She left the house completely. It has been more than two years since this event. I haven't seen Bakhora since the day we officially divorced in court. According to what I heard that she is now living with his brother.

The alarm clock go off. I jump up. I drink my coffee and go to work. It is cloudy. It must have rained during the night, the ground is wet, the golden leaves of the trees are soaked in water, and they hang sadly on the drooping branches. There is a sharp chill in the air, and a thin cloak could not protect him from the sting of the chain. I wonder if I should change into winter clothes in the morning. When I go to the office, no one have come yet. I take the key from the guard and enter the room. It is dark inside. I move the curtain and turn on the light. On my desk is the unfinished report from yesterday waiting to be finished, and next to it is a stack of letters from the organization. Being an assistant to the head of the department, it is my duty to get acquainted with the letters and ensure their execution. I don't have time to review them yesterday. I sit down and sort the letters. After a warning letter from the tax office and small letters from neighboring organizations, an unaddressed envelope arrived. I open the envelope. A letter written in a familiar script :

"Hello, dear!

I brought you greetings from the cold and dry air of the prison. You probably haven't seen those places before. But haven't you forgotten that because of you, someone has to live there and suffer from the punishment?! I went to your friend, whom I once considered my best friend, and told him that he should be afraid to be friends with you. Wish you patience.

Love Someone"

My whole body trembled. Cold sweat begin to break out on my forehead. After all, I don't tell anyone about Zamir, how do this person know?! My legs are shaking, my breathing is quickening, and I can hear my heartbeat.

Who is this person?" Why are they writing me such letters? How does he know secrets that no one else knows? What is the real purpose?

A thousand different questions start spinning in my head. I don't know what to do. "Or from the police?" As soon as this thought came to my mind, the denial flashed out.

No, the police don't sit around like that. If there is any evidence against me, it will be taken away on condition... hurry, what am I saying?! No, no police can arrest me. So what to do now? My first thought is to find the person who wrote this letter. But the fact that the letter had no address blocked my way. Mail does not accept letters without such an address. Therefore, the unknown letter is not delivered by mail. I go to the guard. We both go through the camera footage one by one. But it turn out that no stranger had entered the department since yesterday. No one had even approached my table. I can't get a specific answer even after asking my neighbors. I don't show them what the letter was, but I assume it is related to my personality. A colleague tell me that it is possible to go to the Ministry of Internal Affairs and find out who wrote the letter by the fingerprint left on it. His cousin is an officer. He speake to the his cousin and take the letter and tell him that I should meet him. I go. I don't just take the letter that was left on my desk, but the first letter that come to my house. The paper is examined. After a short examination, the "cousin" led me into his room. I explain the situation. In the guise of a calm but surprised person, I tell the story of the unknown letter that is left at my house. He don't find the situation "serious", apparently he listen to me in an indifferent tone.

– So who wrote the letter to you, did you?

– Yes.

– But it's possible that someone you know wrote it as a joke or to test you, right? Maybe that letter doesn't belong to you at all, maybe it comes to your house by mistake.

– Maybe...

– We do not avoid investigation, but I do not think that this issue is very serious. When the time comes, it will become clear who wrote it and why.

– True, but the fingerprints . . .

– We checked the fingerprints. There are no extraneous traces on the paper except your fingerprints.

I left the Ministry of Internal Affairs. I do not go to the office at all. I go straight home. My head is buzzing. I take medicine and go to bed. Even if I try to sleep, the dangerous thoughts would not let me sleep.

Zamir... nobody knows what happened to him. I think I would take this secret to my grave. So, does anyone else know besides me?! Who could he be? Or is Zamir himself hiring people and trying to make me confess my guilt? If so, the dumpling is considered raw. I would never do that. No one can arrest me. Come on, let them try to find some evidence against me!'

After graduating from the institute, I got a job as an assistant chief accountant in a limited liability company. The chief accountant was much older than me, he was going to retire in two or three years. I worked as an assistant to this person for two years and learned the secrets of the profession. The chief accountant retired, and because I was an exemplary employee, they put me in his place. I started working as in the brochure.

There is a custom among the people: they use the phrase "the devil has gone astray" in relation to a person who is walking on the wrong path. I don't think so. In fact, the devil does not lead a person astray, he lives inside a person from time immemorial. It begins to try to lead a person to his own path even when he has just begun to recognize his senses. The path is chosen at the beginning of life. So, the devil, who has been living inside me for a long time, kept trying to save my ego. I did not return his opinion either. At first, I began to withdraw money from the company's account little by little. Gradually, this amount increased. In the end, I collected everything and bought a house in the city. Then I got married. At the end of the reporting year, I did not report the deficit. But next year, the director changed. After our director said in a meeting that after two or three months, I will retire myself, putting my son in my place, I also got a worm in my bed. If the director changes, my work will be ruined. In any case, I had to think about getting out of here safely. Only if the person who will be put in my place is a fool, he can know my mistakes. All I had to do now was to get someone who didn't know much about the industry to be my assistant. Without a doubt, when I leave, the assistant chief accountant will be appointed. Soon such a person was found. One day I saw my classmate Zamir on the street. Zamir complained that he couldn't find a job. He asked me for help. "Actually, this work is difficult, but I will find a way for you," I said, even though I was a soul inside. Three days later I called. Thus, Zamir started working as an assistant. I had to leave before the director in order not to arouse suspicion. I went to our boss and told him that I wanted to leave and that I had found a job elsewhere. The director did not give up at first. It is hard to find someone who is thorough in his work and "honest" like me. "At least be patient until you find someone to replace you," he said. I recommended Zamir to him. "If you are not satisfied, I will recommend a candidate. Zamir Kadyrov is a person who matches the qualities you mentioned. He has learned a lot even though he has not been on the job for very long. Besides, we are friends with him in life. If he doesn't know something, I will teach him." In this way, I persuaded the chief to leave. You can go wherever you want after the extra–ordinary audit, the director said when I handed him my resignation letter. I spent as much as the price of a car for the lead auditor in charge of the audit. Well, no matter how much I tried, I wanted to remove the "guilt" from myself. Everything was as I expected. Just "lubricating" the head of inspectors so that he wouldn't open at all took more than I thought. Five months after I left, there was no "wind" from Zamir. At the end of the sixth month, I was called to the investigation.

"The case of Zamir Kadyrov is very serious. An audit conducted before he became chief accountant revealed no deficit in the company's accounts. In the audit conducted in the middle of the reporting year after he started his work , there was a large deficit." The conclusion of the inspection when I was leaving the job "shelved" me from guilt. Zamir was locked up. On the day of the last trial, the wife came and said that her husband wanted to meet with me, but I do not go to the court. What do I do there?

It starts to rain outside. The tree branches shake nervously in the wind. The wind forcefully pushed the drops towards the windows. I fell asleep. I don't know how long I slept with that. When I opened my eyes, shivering, the dark room was cold. Every part of my body was shivering from the cold, one eye of the window must have been blown open by the wind, a cold wind was coming from outside. As soon as I lifted my head from the pillow, my vision darkened. I sat on the bed. The problem of my dressing down yesterday is showing all day today. I grabbed the wall and closed the window.

A lonely person should not get sick. In this situation, I can neither make tea nor eat... but my heart misses the sweet food of the house. At this moment, I imagine that there will be hot boiled soup. But there is no ability to prepare it. It hurts me to be thirty-seven and still not have a single friend. My only relative is Rustam, who is walking in his village surrounded by his worries. I spend three more days in this situation. On the fourth day, I start to feel a little better. My colleagues called me in the morning when they notice that I have been absent for three days. I tell them that I will go to work in two or three days. I set out to go to the market to buy ingredients for soup. It is cloudy as always. The sun has not shown its face for almost a week, and the sky, covered with cotton–like clouds, is giving the heart a gloomy, gloomy mood. The bus stopped in front of the market, leaving beautiful buildings behind. I start shopping with meat. I take everything and is leaving when I remembered to buy a lemon. My mother used to make tea with lemon because lemon is good for wind. While I am looking for lemons among the fruit stalls, I suddenly saw Bakhora. My whole body is full of longing mixed with excitement. Bakhora wear a thin coat, a long dress that suited her figure, and her hair was neatly combed. She looks a lot different than the last time I saw her, fuller and more beautiful. I had just taken a couple of steps towards him when she turns around and calls someone. From the neighboring stall, a young man carrying a shopping bag came towards Bakhora. She hands the young man a kilogram of apples in a plastic bag, and they walked past me arm in arm. I am so surprised that I almost dropped the plastic bags in my hand. Bakhora do not even look back at me. As she passed by, I saw that her figure, which was not fully covered by the thin coat he was wearing, showed her pregnancy. "She got married!" "The child is waiting..." I hurried to the station. Until now, my feelings for Bakhora are not clear to me, although I have not missed her even once in the past two years, the way I saw her today, as much as the jealousy that arose in my body when she held that little girl in her arms, the sight that I saw at the end made me so numb. Now I truly realized that I have lost her. My thoughts are interrupted by the voice of the boy conductor:

"Mr, where are you going?"

I was shocked. I looked around, but I could not understand where I was.

"I...I..."

I tell the address.

– Stay out.

I hurriedly got up. The conductor boy helps me carry my shopping bags.

"Thank you, brother." Be healthy.

"It's not worth it." You will be my uncle, it will be a shame if I don't help, – he smiles sincerely.

"Your uncle?" – I repeat questioningly.

– Yes, I am the son of your friend Zamir. You used to visit us a lot.

Embarrassment burned my whole body. I could not look into the child's eyes. I just mumbled.

– Is your dad, right?

– Yes, it's fine. Now they have released it to the "column". We are going to see. Soon he will come out.

– Did you go to work? – I asked, surprised by his profession, which did not suit his short stature.

– Yes.

In his voice there is a calm, serious thoughtfulness characteristic of adults. He can not be called a child from his words.

– What grade do you study in? What's going on at your school?

– I study in the seventh grade. Our class is in the afternoon. I just work until class time.

He looks down guiltily.

– I should help and look after my mother...my siblings are still small...

I don't remember how I get home. My eyes are open, but I can't see anything. My heart beats but I feel nothing. It is as if I am completely cut off from this world. When I close my eyes, my mother's stern face appears in front of me.

– Mother!

The fact that I didn't go to see him even once in the last month, that I barely made it to his funeral, that I spent three days there, and that I went back to the city... all of this made the burden of my guilt even heavier. Who I am? Why did I come to this world, what did I do?

An envelope float from the gap between the closed room door and the floor and stops at my feet. There is no sound from the hallway. I know very well who the letter is from. I open the notebook without haste. Familiar note:

Hi!

I came!

Someone

I laugh. I laugh as loud as I could, clutching my stomach. My voice sound like I am screaming. The walls echoed with laughter. I laugh even more when I see that even the cracked walls of this narrow balcony could echo. The window is just open. The cold air mix with the smell of rain from outside was closing in. The screeching sounds of the cars crawling like mice below, combine with the pattering of raindrops, made me sad. The intensity of the rain increase, it begins to pour in buckets. Suddenly someone's sharp eyes catch my eye. A strong lightning flash and the surroundings lit up for a moment. Now I see that the light of lightning cannot be like that of the sun. It becomes clear that what I had longed for as light all my life was actually the light of lightning that flashed only once and then went out, the real light is in the sun. Now I realize that nothing can be denied. Someone is still staring at me. His eyes, looking at me, his face remind me of someone. I stare at him with all my attention...

I recognize him! I feel very happy at that moment. I felt a kind of relief in my body. I stretch out my hands towards him and take a step forward. Someone come to me... There is a muted lightning flash in the sky. A flash of lightning flashed in the darkness of the black clouds and immediately go out...

BREAD

In the dusk of the evening, the old man entered through the gate leading his son. The old woman's eyes were on them.

– Hey, what did they say?" she asked impatiently.

– It didn't work...it must have been fixed.

– Didn't tell that he has a young family and started his son's wedding in the fall.

– I wonder, if the chairman would understand this. Saifullah's youngest son was taken away one month before her wedding. Be thankful, Yusuf managed to get married and have a child anyway...

– When are you leaving now?

– The day after tomorrow.

The old woman and her daughter–in–law start packing a travel bag for her son early in the morning. She washes the old clothes and mends them. The four grandchildren keep asking questions from all sides: "Grandma, where is dad going?". Let's play together." The old man enters the door. "Tursunmurad has come. Let's slaughter the lamb." The old woman takes one look at Tursunmurad, who is sharpening a knife, and looks twice at the old man. "Let's start the wedding..."

"Don't be greedy, old woman. Your only son is going to war. After he comes back, he will feed a hundred of them."

A cauldron boils in the middle of the yard. Relatives from far and near come. Everyone says the same thing.

In the evening, everyone disperses. The old woman is lying on the couch with her son in her arms. She sits next to her son. "Yusuf, get up, my son, go to your place and sleep." The son is silent. You will leave tomorrow. Sleep with your children today."

The old woman gives the old man a seat on the platform.

– We need to bake bread tomorrow. There isn't even a pinch of flour left on the top. Can't we buy the meat for it?

– It's morning. I'll take it from Tursun.

The old woman wakes up in the dark of the morning. She reads the morning. She prays to God that her son will arrive safely and return safely, and that the scourge of war will be averted... The old woman sifted flour and made dough for the two dishes she brought to the meat. She made soft bread, the oven heats up. In the hot oven, she covers the bread with two sides of the cake.

The train whistles. "Let's go, say goodbye." The old woman pats her son on the shoulder, who is standing like a goose in front of him. may this fate bind you."

– Goodbye, again, stay well, I will write a letter.

The train beeps twice. The boy looks back and gets on the train. The train moves away. The old woman clutches the bitten bread in her hand and her son falls on the path.

Fortunately, the bread is hung on a nail on the wall. Every time the old woman looks at the bread, she remembers her son.

A year has passed since then. Nasiba's bread hardens like a stone, its color fades, but it still reminds the memory of her only child. The old woman reads the letters from her son under the wall where the bread is hanging. She doesn't know why she does this...

On the other hand, that year will come hard. It's a harsh winter, there's no bread to eat, everyone is hungry. How many people died of swelling after eating kunjara. There was nothing left to eat porridge and soup. The old man went to collect firewood in the valley. Grandchildren go here and there. "Grandma, we're hungry," "Grandma, food." The old woman is depressed. This situation has been going on for a week. The saltiness is making it difficult for the children. Until now, they have been tricking her with porridge, it's been three days. It's over. "Grandma, bread." The youngest granddaughter stretches her hand to the bread hanging on the wall. "Grandma, give me some bread." The old woman looks at the bread on the wall and her grandchild who is stuttering... "Forgive me, my son!"

Boil water in the sand and pour boiling water over the nasiba bread. "Wait a minute, my children. Let the bread soften." Children are happy. Seeing the joy in their eyes, the old woman washes her face... Looking at her grandchildren, who are sleeping and chewing bread, she thinks: "Forgive me, my son. I have no other choice. If God has added your portion here, you will surely come and eat your portion. You just have to come back, my child. God, come back safely. On the day of my return, I will cover two ovens with such bread. That's when you'll eat your lot, my son, then you'll definitely eat it!'

MY EYES ARE ON YOUR HEART

When Lobar go to the courtyard, the day have already spread, the sun is spreading its golden rays evenly across the clear sky, and a gentle breeze is blowing. As she walked towards the infirmary, he glanced at the farm. Oh, it's a pity, instead of the potatoes, which she had finished chopping only yesterday, there were green bushes, and between the leaves, there were ripe strawberries, shining like pearls in the sunlight. Lobar's eyes sparkled. She really loves strawberries. It was good.

He picked a handful of strawberries, and someone called "Lobar" after him. A familiar voice...

– Lobar, please get up. Milk the cow before dawn.

Lobar wake up startled. The body of her mother–in–law could be seen through the slightly opened door. Then she recognizes, it was dream.

– Now, mom. – she says, embarrassed that she had fallen asleep.

She washes quickly and took the bucket and went to the farm. As she passes the farm, she deliberately stopps and looks in the direction where the potatoes are planted. On the wet furrows, potato stalks were swaying in the wind. Lobar sighs inwardly. Although the fact that potatoes turn into strawberries is a counterintuitive phenomenon, but at the same time, she really wants this miracle to happen.

When Lobar returns from milking the cow, the mother–in–law, who had been snowing since morning, is putting the blankets on the cow.

– Give it to me, mom, – says Lobar, reaching for the blanket in his mother–in–law's hand.

– Look at the tea. It may have boiled and dried up.

Lobar run to the kitchen. Quickly sets the table. She heats food for his father–in–law. On the table, the they drink tea in silence. At that moment, Lobar begin to think about her husband Adkham. Her husband, who has been driver, has gone to the neighboring village for a week. He said he will return in two weeks.

Although it has been more than five months since Lobar became a bride to this family, Adkham has never been away from work for such a long period of time. That's why Lobar is somber. Adkham calls every two or three days, and even then, the connection is not good, and the conversation is not heard properly, and it is immediately disconnected. He also called yesterday and said something. But Lobar could not advance. While she is digging half a cup of milk in the midst of these thoughts, she involuntarily remembered the strawberries she had seen in her dream. At the same time, she really wants to eat even just one strawberry.

– I will go to the market today. If you make a list of anything you need, I would bring it. – said his father-in-law as he get up.

– Lobar, come in quickly and take out a pen and paper, – ordered the mother-in-law.

Lobar take a paper and sit down next to her mother-in-law. Perhaps, she will ask me if she needs something, she said to her mother-in-law with hope. As for the mother-in-law, she began to make a list without even caring about her daughter-in-law. As always, the most necessary items for livelihood were written first, and the more necessary items were written second, but neither the mother-in-law nor the father-in-law said, "Lobar, don't you need anything?" Lobar stares at his father-in-law as he folds the list into four and put it in his pocket. As always, the father–in–law put on his shoes without haste, and his expression is calm. Feeling that hope is futile, Lobar go into the kitchen without saying a word. She laughs inwardly. Her eyes filled with tears. For some reason, the times in her father's house came to mind. She remembered how her father would ask each family member "what do you need" one by one before going to the market, and everything the girl wanted would be provided in front of her in the blink of an eye. A pang of longing filled her body.

During the day, Lobar is in a tired mood. She lost her appetite and did not eat properly. All she needed is strawberries. She tries to eat a little jam to make up for it, but it doesn't work. Nothing beats strawberries.

It is late. Lobar prepares the dinner. The three of them ate without saying a word. She made tea for the mother–in–law and father–in–law and arranged the work in the kitchen. Her mother–in–law shivering from the cold, go in to sleep. Lobar is left alone in the yard. She stared for a long time at the picture of a strawberry on the table, which had been lowered into the belly of the teapot. She remember the dream she had today again.

The wind pick up. Lobar cleans the table and enters her room. She stretches out comfortably. As soon as she closes her eyes, she pushes away the image of red strawberries that appeares before her eyes. "That's enough, let's go. I won't eat anyway." Lobar's eyes fell asleep. Strawberries leave her alone for a moment. She was just starting to dream again when she heards a soft click on the window pane. Lobar wake up startled. The window clicks twice more. She hastily raises the curtain. Adkham is standing behind the window with a half-smile on her sun-darkened face. "Wow," Lobar says with surprise and joy. Adkham gestures with his hand to open the window. As soon as Lobar openes the window, cool air enteres the room. The chandeliers on the ceiling swayed. The wind brought a sweet smell mixed with the smell of oil. Lobar\ looks at her husband questioningly. Adkham carefully places the basket on the windowsill.

– This is for you.

Curiously, Lobar reaches out and gently pick it up. In the basket, it is red like a pearl in the moonlight there are strawberries…

THE NINTH SQUARE

Let me be free, my heart! "Free your fingers, give them freedom. Maybe this freedom will make me free from you too... I would like not to recognize the memories. I wish I didn't love rain, I wish I hated coffee without sugar, I wish I never went to that coffee shop..."

It was raining. Drops pouring to fill the empty space of the heart. A rainy Sunday in October. The smell of rain in the air was so depressing that a young man without a raincoat carrying a leather briefcase was walking alone on the path in this weather, when he came to a coffee shop on the side of the road and stopped. . He hesitantly entered the door, patted the drops on the threshold with his palms and sat down on one of the empty seats. The waitress appeared in front of the girl as soon as she settled down .

– Coffee without sugar, with a glass of warm water – he said while flipping through his notebook.

– Maybe I'll give you something sweet to cut the bitter taste?

– A glass of water! – he repeated.

The waitress immediately disappeared . Zoom soon brought "unique" orders. Black coffee without sugar and a glass of warm water...

While the young man began to puzzle over the answers of the unknown number of X, he did not even notice the ghost of a person approaching him. "If the x–square is added to the x–square, then the square root..."

–Excuse me...

Raised his head, surprised by an unfamiliar voice that disturbed his attention. A pretty girl was standing in front of the table .

–Is this the ninth table?

The young man hesitated and looked at the paper stuck to the forehead of the table . The number "9" was written there.

– Well, – he said more painfully.

– Was supposed to see you, right? We talked yesterday. You wanted to sell me a painting...

– I think you made me look like someone, I...

– I can't compare people to someone. This is table 9 and you said yesterday that you would be at table 9 at exactly 11 o'clock.

The girl pushed the chair in front of him and sat down.

– Well, where is Volkova's "Night Rain"?

The young man was confused for a while, not knowing what to do. He opened both his palms in the air and shrugged.

–As you can see, I'm just a normal person working on quadratic equations. As for table 9, I came and sat because this place was empty .

The girl narrowed her brown eyes and looked better at the boy's face. When he realized that the person he was looking for was not him, he stood up in shock.

– Sorry, I was wrong. I'm sorry if I disturbed you ...

The girl apologized again and again and sat down at one of the empty tables. And the young man began to find the solution of quadratic equations. Usually, when he got down to something, he was so obsessed that he forgot about the people around him. This time, after an hour of hard work, the fourth solution of x was finally found. He walked out of the coffee shop with the relief of a man relieved of a heavy burden. It was drizzling outside, and the bus stop next to the open space near the coffee shop was drenched in the rain. The young man walked straight to the station. Since it was Sunday , there were few people on the street. At the station , there was no one except the girl who was quietly watching the cars passing by and returning from the street with her umbrella folded into a "cane" in her hand . He stood at the corner of the station and waited for the bus.

– Excuse me, can you tell me the number of the coming bus?

"Nine," he said, looking casually at the girl standing next to him.

The girl said thank you and got on the bus. While the young man was alone at the station, he began to think about where he had seen the familiar face of the girl . After a second , something flashed in his mind . It was her: the girl he met in the coffee shop. As soon as he remembered the girl, he involuntarily remembered the conversation that had taken place . A girl who came to buy a painting of a certain artist about the rain... If she didn't look better then, the girl's eager face had a kind of sincerity that was not found in others...

For the next week, he worked exclusively in the library. The research work is almost ready. If he works hard, he can graduate in three months. After that, you can see that he will become a candidate of science . The next Sunday it rained again . As if nature had become accustomed to it, every Saturday evening, the air was covered with cotton clouds, and it rained in the evening. Naturally, the sweet sleep of Sunday morning was disturbed by the mist of raindrops. Apartment on the fourth floor. The young students staying in the next room sleep until noon on weekends. The young man had breakfast, put on his autumn cloak, and went on his way with a notebook and a thick book of Fichtengols in his arms.

The cold, damp air was blowing outside, which gave the heart a nighttime mood. He entered his favorite coffee shop. His feet led him to the 9th table by himself. That artist girl was sitting across the table .

−Sorry to bother you. May I sit here?

The girl was startled as if she was lost in imagination.

if I scared you .

A smile spread across the girl's cheeks.

– It's okay, sit down.

– You didn't recognize me when... – he said, sitting opposite the girl.

The girl thought for a while. His forehead twitched and he was trying to remember.

– Sorry, I didn't recognize you.

We met you last week in this cafe . Mistaking me for some artist…

"I remembered," said the girl with a half smile. – you are that – Mr. Mathematician.

– He is the one – said the young man with a laugh. – But how did you know that I am a mathematician?

– On that day, you talked about some equations.

– Yes, as a matter of fact, I have not yet reached the level of mathematics. I am an independent researcher at the university. So what about you? If

I'm not mistaken, you came to meet some artist then?

– Erkin Akmalov, – said the girl with special emphasis, – is a wonderful artist. I wanted to buy a copy of Yelena Volkova's painting from him. "Night Rain" is simply a masterpiece. I am also an artist. It is my dream to paint this picture.

– By the way, what was your name?

– My name Masuma.

– Well, Masuma, did you buy that picture?

– No, – he said, playing with the handle of the cup on the table with his thin fingers .

– Why?

– He brought another photo. I was just asking for "Night Rain" .

– Are you still waiting for that person?

– No, he did not draw the work I was looking for. They were just wrong.

– Then draw it yourself. After all, you are an artist.

Masuma stared at the coffee in the cup for a long time.

– My eyes do not see well. " It's been a long time since I left without painting," he said with a sigh.
– Even in glasses, the colors fade, not to mention the lines ...

The young man could not say anything. He is not a person who consoles anyone in his life, he cannot say anything if someone feels sorry for something or cries in front of him.

– Would you like to order something?

The arrival of the waitress cleared to the awkward situation.

– Coffee without sugar.

The waiter immediately prepared the order.

– Why do you drink coffee without sugar?

Masuma looked at the young man from the window. When he spoke to the person in front of him, he looked at the target roughly, and the reason why his eyes never met the young man's gaze seemed to be clear . All together , warm feelings began to awaken in the young man's heart. He wondered why he was speaking so "openly" to a strange girl, contrary to his habit.

– I don't like sweet taste. My brain works better with spicy coffee. Besides, I don't get distracted.

– Don't shy away from sweets. Your mood will be depressed by night. You will drift away from the memories.

– I have no memories to tell. Longing to remember. Since I was born, I have been like a character in a pre–written story. I was born, I went to school. As the eldest grandson of my grandfather, who was a doctor of mathematics at the university, it was already predicted that I would become a mathematician. Here, I am still busy learning the mysteries of mathematics. My brothers have their own families. Your life, worries... Here, for example, you, tell me. How do you feel in a place where you are not known?

– Of course, good. As long as my absence is not known, then my presence is not known. This will ensure that you are free during that period. In any case, this is not a tragedy.

– True . It is not known whether I am around my family. I think they take it for granted that I live far away. I have been living away from home since I was ten years old. First in science school, then lyceum, university, work... I 'm probably the only one who feels like an outsider in the family circle ...

– Why don't you alienate yourself from your own mother?

He could not answer the girl's question. He never told almost anyone that Ayisi was not his mother. Besides, he didn't want to tell Ma'suma about his pain all of a sudden. The girl seemed to notice it too and changed the question.

Do you like mathematics ?

– I didn't know that, I couldn't even imagine who I would be if it wasn't for him .

– You are just used to mathematics. There's a difference between liking things and being attached to…

– Great ideas. But I am a scientist. I only believe in things that have clear proof. What you say is all relative sentiments.

– So you don't believe in feelings, do you?

"That's right," said the young man while sipping coffee.

– So tell me, have you ever tried to solve equations or problems that have not been solved so far?

– Of course.

– For example?

– Do you know how to play chess? – the young man suddenly turned the conversation in another direction.

– I know.

– So, you know how the grain of the queen goes. Queen is the strongest piece on the chessboard. Unlike any other piece, it can move vertically, horizontally and diagonally. Have you ever thought? How many pieces can be placed on one chessboard in such a way that they cannot attack each other?

–An interesting question...–Ma'suma furrowed her eyebrows a little and began to think.

"Eight," the young man continued solemnly. – The fact is that 8 pieces can be placed on a standard 64–square chessboard without being attacked by one of the other. It turns out that there are 92 suitable configurations of this method. You know what I tried ?

–Find the ninety–third of those configurations?

– No, – the young man knocked the cup that was sitting in his hand and put it in place, – I wanted to find a way to place the ninth queen . For this, I certainly did not use boards and pieces.

Curiosity began to shine in Masuma's eyes. He was now listening to the young man so intently that his cup of coffee was half cooled.

Can be found simply using matrices . But a scientist named Simkin found an approximate way to arrange n such farzins on an n by n square chessboard without attacking each other. That is, by simply multiplying that number n by 0.143n with formulas. This is the minimum number of possible configurations.

– So, did that scientist find the solution before you?

– No, it's just that Simkin set a bigger goal than me and strived for it. Of course, it is impossible not to acknowledge the knowledge of a scientist. But the solution he found has not yet been fully tested by the mathematicians of the world.

– Maybe that 9th piece can be solved without all the formulas, just with the board.

–No. Everything in mathematics is based on formulas, theories that require exact proof. Also, I tried hard to solve it the "peasant" way you mentioned . It is not possible. For the 9th farzin, it is necessary to add the 9th row and the square . I just tried the impossible...

if not emotion ?

– This is just curiosity.

– Maybe you won't know when the time comes. I could not explain to you? Masuma said with a sarcastic smile.

– It's like I don't understand Volkova's "Night Rain"?

– You...– The girl's eyelashes fluttered, – do you know that picture?

– I searched on the Internet the same day I met you.

Masuma did not say a word. He just sighed deeply. He looked at the window. Then he stopped for a while when he came to the drops, to the coffee cup on the table , and asked:

– So, what do you think about the picture ?

A picture with all sorts of paints thrown around . It is difficult to understand. I saw only the traces of drops. In general, it is a characteristic of artists to imitate something. You imitate the beauty of nature.

– Maybe you are right. But under each imitation something is created...

– It's a good thing...

Masuma smiles. His smile was as pure and sincere as his eyes.

– Now I have to go.

He stood up deftly.

– Maybe I will follow you?

–Thank you. I can catch up. Bye Bye.

He began to worry that his last words had offended the girl .

He never saw Ma'suma again after that. During the next three months, he was busy preparing for the defense . In the meantime, he submitted a document to one of the foreign research centers. A month after the defense, a positive response letter arrived. He was accepted as a researcher. He put aside his university work and began to prepare for his departure. The visa issue did not take long . After three weeks, he was going to fly . Meanwhile, he stayed in the village for a while. When he returned to the city, it was two days before his departure .

It was a sunny spring Sunday. The young man wanted to see the destinations that were dear to him , so he went for a walk. He went to the same coffee shop where he met Masuma. Table 9 is busy. He went further and sat down. The waiter ordered the young man a coffee without sugar and began to silently watch the raindrops falling on the busy life of the city from the window . Frankly, the bitterness that was gnawing at his heart at that time could be removed by the bitter taste of coffee. While he was staring at the window where the drops were hitting one after another, he started thinking about Masuma for some reason. At that moment, both eyes were on the door as if the girl was coming in. But he finished drinking coffee without sugar , the person he was waiting for did not appear, and table 9 was not free. The guy left the cafe. His feet led him to the garden on the other side of the road .

Although spring has arrived, the weather is still cold. For this reason, there were few people in the garden. Except for the occasional arm–in–arm couple dating, the gates of the art museum, which adjoined an almost empty garden courtyard, were crowded with people. The young man involuntarily walked towards the museum. At the gate of the museum hung a poster about a general exhibition of modern artists . As soon as he entered the exhibition hall, he felt as if he had entered into the bosom of a place full of secrets.

the exhibition where the creative works of today's modern artists were displayed, he involuntarily stopped in front of a familiar painting. It was "Night Rain" by Elena Volkova. Then he remembered Masuma. Some kind of reflections randomly drawn among the black colors, traces left by drops – night rain. No rain is depicted in the photo. Only the trail left by the drops on the glass can remind of the rain. Masuma considered this painting a masterpiece for him. As he stared at it carefully, some lines began to take the place of the blur in the picture. It was as if something had progressed . But the young man's thoughts were interrupted by the voice of a museum employee, who was telling a group of young men and women about the paintings, five steps away.

– What you are looking at is Masuma Asror's "9–square". At first glance, the picture shows a chess piece. But for some reason alone, other grains and cells are not visible. A lone square checker and a lone queen grain…

At that moment, time seemed to stop . The young man pushed past the crowd and came to the picture .

Illustration of a black square checker in the corner of a chessboard over a dark space. Above him is a white queen grain. Shadows of other grains can be seen in the space. Looking carefully, he saw that they were all queens. The 9th square and the 9th square against the background of the unknown, shadows and ghosts of the eight queens... Something stung in the young man's chest . It's as if deep–seated memories are resurfacing, old wounds are reopening...

He lived without wanting to admit these memories. But in the current situation, he gave up. Surrender to those memories that once boasted of not wanting to remember anything... Now what... can he forget them to the extent that he no longer recognizes them, can he get rid of the haunting of so many memories and incomprehensible experiences from a single conversation ?! Can he escape?! …

BEFORE AND AFTER

BEFORE

Everything we see exists between beginning and end. Between these two destinations, existence passes the so-called path. So are humans. Some see it as fate. But destiny is pre-existing, pre-existing, and post-presence. Otherwise, what does the human soul live for? Do you know why I said it's the spirit and not the human race?! I think you know. If you are still the one I know, you know.

The wind scatters soil particles into the air, dust covers the earth and sky, and the sky shrinks. A tiny piece is cut off from somewhere on the earth's surface. Then that piece rises into the air, disappears into the clouds, but will return someday, because he knows that only he can fill that broken heart. You think it all starts there, but the beginning was before that...

They say that people are lines. One is crooked, one is straight, one is close, the other is far. Wherever the lines begin, life begins there, and at some point the two lines will meet at the zero point. But there is another thing that does not correspond to this essence: according to science, the lines have no end, they continue to infinity. And then I understand why you keep talking about the soul, because the human soul is eternal. And life is just his "journey" on Earth for a certain period of time. Now I understand the words of our geography teacher, "The Earth consists of spatial points of the lines between the two poles"...

I didn't like geography before. As soon as I heard the name of science, all I could think of were the blank maps that I painted without sleeping all night, my reddened eyes staring at the atlas, my gold armor that I was afraid of losing, and the notes of the evil teacher. As the various colors go from satin to map with my blunt pencils that go over and over on the white paper, a reddish color enters my colorless eyes.

At the time, I didn't quite understand what the purpose of transferring the paint from the atlas to the map without writing was. One day I asked our teacher about it . The teacher laughed at my question and opened the atlas on my desk and asked:

– What are you looking at?

– The Earth.

– What about here?

The teacher's finger was fixed on the map without writing.

– I see the Earth.

– What's the difference?

– One colored, one colorless.

The teacher now opened the painted page of the map without writing.

– What is the difference with this?

– Both are colorful, but not exactly the same.

– Each of you has been given one world, – said our teacher, turning to the class. – You give it your own color. While coloring, you will learn what color it is, but do not forget one thing: in the end, the world of thirty students will turn out to be thirty different. It's true that in the atlas you paint where the paint is given with a paintbrush, red on red, green on green, but everyone's pencil is different...

So gradually I started to like this science. After that, it's up to you to choose a field. And the reason for this is that teacher. When we were tired of drawing maps without notes and the regular classes started to get boring, our teacher would carefully take out his book with tattered pages in a blue volume from his bag. reads stories. These stories will be about unknown distant Africa, America, Australia – the mysterious lands behind the ocean and their nature, the mysterious islands where the heroes have gone, their rare nature, jaguars and cougars who fought one–on–one. but it became loud and crawled into our ears. The whole class was quiet as if water had been poured, and we listened to the teacher with our whole bodies. I do not remember the name of the book and the author. But it is because of that teacher's book that threatens to tear out our ears if we are careless in my choice of geography.

Sit still, or I'll go and take off your earrings right now!

Didn't you prepare for the lesson? Well, you'll go home without a earrings today!

At first, as soon as I heard these threats from our teacher, I was afraid of what would happen if I entered the house without my earrings. The teacher did not carry out the threat that he makes every time he gets angry.

Gradually I grew up. Those ears are now small to my ears. Grandma taking off and putting on another:

– All right, my daughter! Don't take it off until your father brings you something more valuable than this, – said and carefully putting it in my ear as if it were something.

– Say not your father, but the bird you caught, mom, she has become a big girl now, – my aunt said.

"There is still time until the bird catches." Until then, let him walk like this.

At that time I had no idea what it was all about...

***

In the beginning you were given beautiful wings. Such beautiful wings that I have seen pictures of in books, they resemble those of the legendary hawk. Golden feathers like dice are scattered in the sun, and when they rub against each other, fire is formed. I know how many great flights await you in these wings. And my wings are a little heavy. It was always difficult for me to fly. A few heavy rings were also hung. Heavy rings, bad rings. I can't seem to get rid of them.

Have you ever heard the song of the phoenix?! It is said that phoenix only smokes before his death. When the golden wings are spread wide and their moans reach their peak, fire starts to burn from their wings. Phoenix continues to smoke until the last bit of sound burns out. In the end, only a pile of embers will remain...

AND

And from that ember, another qaqnus appears and continues the life of the previous phoenix. Thus existence continues to live in it. I exist in this moment and it lives in me. So, when some fire burned down, the relic of it was transferred to me and is with me now. You also have a "Now" that precedes the "Then" you always think about. Between before and then there is always now. It is the only fiber that binds and separates the first and the next at the same time...

When I was in college, I had a groupmate. The first time I saw this girl, I remembered her ears. From the soft part of the ear to the top, I don't know how many, it was filled with earrings. Then I was able to count the first time that girl got on the board: she was carrying twelve earrings, six in each ear. In time, when that girl became the first of the group to be engaged, the seventh joined those wise men. Even when it was the seventh, it was obvious that it was the biggest, heaviest, and most expensive. "May your bird be happy," congratulated my friends. At first I didn't understand, then suddenly I remembered what my aunt and grandmother said when she put a new zirak in my ear, and everything became clear...

In time, I completely gave up those gold rings. I hid it in one of the jars that were stored in our glass cabinet, which was given to me as a dowry by my mother. Grandma "Where are your earrings?" I said, "I lost it."

It's funny, people who didn't even notice that I was wearing it, now ask why I don't have ears. You appeared after I got rid of those rings. We have never met before. It is true that we existed before and will continue to exist. Don't worry, as long as there are "nows", this existence will live on. And as long as those "nows" exist, the paths will never meet.

The day I took off my glasses, I looked in the mirror, watched my empty ears for a while, and when I took a picture, the face I was looking at in the mirror was not mine. I got scared, closed my eyes with my hands and opened them again after a moment. Still a different look, a different look. That was the first time we met you. And after that, whenever I want to see you, I just need to look in the mirror until later.

Even when I was still a student, I worked at the school and every time I entered the class, I remembered that book of our geography teacher, when I could not find the lost light in the eyes of my students, the interest in science. I knew I would have to find it in the book anyway, but it hurt that I couldn't remember the author or the name. "I wish I could find just one copy of it and read it to my students in my classes, so that they may have even the slightest interest in the mysterious world of geography, even if the pages try and turn yellow. ," I sighed to myself.

But without a thousand searches, without going through various bookstores, that book would never have been found. Every time I passed by the bazaar in Kazirabad, I used to rub the neck of the old Russian bookseller and rummage through his books. Sellers used to say that there is no point in looking for a book whose name is complete, or at least the author is not remembered. And the book was silent, as if it was looking for a way to hide from me in a thousand different ways. And I wanted to look for it, even though I knew it wouldn't be found. But then I thanked myself for not finding the book. If that book had been found, we would never have met you...

AFTER

People are sent to each other either as a test or as a test. We make the mistake of thinking that tests are tests and tests are tests. Are you my test or my dick?! This is a secret to me. And it always remained a secret. My secret that will continue, the secret that I kept from everyone and eventually kept from me. The truth is locked in an old chest, chained with rings, no one knows what's inside. The mystery left in the dusty books on the library shelves...

I was disturbed by the ghost of the conductor, who flew by like the wind.

Train, roads. Where am I going? Road, road, road. If there are roads, then there are long dreams. I was looking out the window at the scenery that was lined up like a chain, trying to remember everything from the beginning, when my companion next to me got into a conversation.

– I'm sorry, didn't you study in fourty second school?

I studied, I spent exactly 9 years of my life in and out of that school. There I learned to read and write, and of course geography. From the conversation, it became clear that this person, who is 4–5 years older than me, and the clothes he was wearing was a bit ill–fitting, is the son of our geography teacher, whose grave is full of light. To be sure, something broke inside me, something burned. What was broken was the fear of never finding that book, but the hope of finding the next one. I asked her about her mother's book. The boy did not remember. No matter how many ways I described it, he kept smiling. I explained that I really needed that book, and that it would do me a lot of good if I could at least find the author and the name.

– I will check when I go home, if you leave your number, I can let you know the result. – he said.

Then three days later I got a call.

– I found what you were looking for!

I wish you knew how happy I was at that moment. I was so excited that I dropped the phone in my hand.

– If you tell me the name, I would write it down.

– Well, how about you put it. Since it is an old book, no one needs it in our house anyway. Help yourself, you may take it away.

As excited as I was to hear that the book had been found, the fact that it could now be mine doubled, if not quadrupled my excitement. Forgetting to say thank you in my happiness, I said "now, now" and got dressed and went on my way.

And finally, the said address. A red door, a log house, an ancient thing like pepper beads that filled the house. A young woman opened the door. My teacher must have a daughter–in–law, I thought to myself: she is about the same age as me, maybe younger than me. I went inside with a woman's gesture. We settled down on one side of the bed placed in the bright and cozy living room. At that moment, my teacher's son came out of the other room smiling, holding that blue book in his hand:

– Here is the book you were looking for!

Yes, it was the same, the pages were tattered, maybe because most of them were torn out, the book did not fit the thick cover, it was kind of sloppy, and the writing on the face could not be read even after trying.

The boy handed the book to me, I carefully opened it as if it were a gift, and the place where the author and book title were written on the first page was torn out. I looked for the back. It's the same there. It seems to me that someone did it on purpose.

"I'll tell you a secret, just keep it between us," began the boy who was watching my actions. – This book was written by my mother herself. It's hard to believe at first glance, but it's true. My mother always tried to hide it from everyone. I don't know where the book is, how many copies it was published. I did not understand at all how my mother wrote it and why she hid it by writing it down. When you asked me on the train, I pretended I didn't remember, but I knew you were talking about this book. Only after so many years, I was surprised that this book written by my mother, which she put on paper with her own hands, is being remembered so much. I was a bit angry at first, but then I think it's better that it is useful to someone than sitting on the edge of a shelf collecting dust.

I left my teacher's house more relaxed. There were many unanswered questions. I may never get the answers. I realized: that book can never be mine. Because I didn't get it. Yes, I drowned the couple in a sea of wonder and left the book in the hands of the boy. Just a quick, "Thanks, but I can't take it, bye" and I came back.

I hate hearing footsteps coming back because they always take something away from you. If those people are with you, then another.

After this incident, I thought that I would be like a person who has lost his great purpose in life, but such a calmness took over my whole soul that I did not even understand why. In such days, You got out of my way and the worlds, before, after, and roads began to change differently.

I often went to the library of the institute to prepare lessons when I left work early. I didn't like to go to the room early in the morning and join in the conversations of the girls about who they saw in the park today with whom, and about the dowry they were collecting for their unmarried marriage. As usual, I was writing a synopsis while wearing headphones and listening to music, when the lady on duty came and warned me that they would be closing in 5 minutes. Only then I raised my head and looked around: there was no one left. I hurriedly went to the window where the librarian was sitting, handed over the book and took back my library ID card. It seems that he was waiting for me, as soon as I left the door, the guard uncle shouted and locked the door from the inside. But at that moment, it seemed that for some reason my better library ticket was exchanged for a new one. When I opened it and looked inside: number 127 . Everything is clear: mine was number 27. The librarian was wrong. When I tried to go back, they locked the door. As soon as I went, the librarian aunt gave me the latest certificate on the table. The mistake started with me. In fact, my library ticket was seized by him. Better yet, I thought it would be more useful to go tomorrow to the faculty where this student studies and find him.

But as I got wrapped up in some work, I completely forgot about this incident, and I only remembered when I was going to the library to write an independent work on natural landscapes the next week.

After a short inquiry at the dean's office, I managed to find him. The young man didn't understand anything at first, it seems, he was staring at the certificate in one hand and at me.

– Please look at your ticket. It should be mine.

– You know, I... still. To be honest... since I have the ticket, I hardly go to the library. My brother sometimes uses it. I think he must have gone that day. If you don't really need it, can I bring it tomorrow?

– Can't you find that brother now?

– Unfortunately, no. He doesn't study here. You better not go after school tomorrow. If it is true, I will take it to you myself.

***

In the beginning you were given a pure heart. I don't care what other people think, I still call you good. It doesn't really matter what you look like, you're just one of the good people I've seen after, if not the only one. While I am addressing you as you, in real life I would say neither you nor you. It seems that the pronouns in our language could not express the attitude towards you. Because both you and you are used in the second person. But I never saw you as the second person in front of me...

– Why do you always read the same book? It seems that you want to write a scientific paper about Halit? – you say, pointing to a geographical encyclopedia as thick as a pillow in my hand. (Since then, since the day you came to return my library ID and apologized repeatedly for the carelessness that caused the misunderstanding, if we meet in the library, say hello briefly late)

– Just curiosity. I read a book when I was young. Rather, they threatened and...

And I'll start talking about that blue book. I went to my teacher's house looking for it and returned without it. There is a lot of similar information and scientific facts in my dictionary, and I am collecting sources for myself after reading it – all of them. I think you will be surprised to hear why I went out without taking my teacher's book. I even expect a standard answer from you: "Why did you throw it away after searching so much? You should take the book, read it to your students for the sake of your teacher's memory, and maybe you should have revealed the author and republished it." But on the contrary, to my surprise, you remain silent for a while and say:

– You did it right.

– Isn't it?! Now I was preparing myself to listen.

– No, why now? Disclosure of the book would not be fair to that teacher. In any case, if he hid it all his life, then he had a good reason.

– I'm sorry, but it still amazes me how he manages to write such vividly illustrated stories.

– What's wrong? A man can do what a man does. If you try, you too can write such a book.

– That's a bit over the top, – I say, laughing.

– No, it did not exceed. You don't know what you can do yet. All people are like that. But remember, you can write a better one if you need to. How old were you the last time you were read that book?

– Thirteen, maybe fourteen.

– That book was the best for thirteen–year–old you. Maybe when you read it now, it seems very simple and lively. Maybe that's why your teacher hides it from others and only teaches it to children?! Just stay with yourself and think it through.

– What does it mean to be alone with yourself?

– Don't you know? After all, it's nice to be standing – you say with a smile, – even if there are many people around you, you can be alone with yourself. If you give your soul free rein, just let it go. Let him go where he wants. Then you will be alone with yourself.

– With a body without a soul?

– Not with a body, of course, let your heart stay with you. I said free your soul, not your heart. For example, I feel so free every time I come to the library. There are many people here, but there are more books than them. Only here I can understand the real essence of my scientific work. Just think about it. A person should not be afraid to succeed.

– I wasn't afraid then, I just didn't believe in myself. Then I spoke about it.

– Two weeks later, we met again in the library. I had that book in my hand.

– So, have you thought about it?

– Yes.

– Twenty years from now, wouldn't some of your readers be looking for your book that they don't know the name of?

– Searches, only by author and name!

– Good job!

So you go to the empty seats in the back. And I am devoted to reading. Only the whisper of the pages fills the silence. I don't even notice how time has passed.

I don't know what was given to me at first. It is clear that I did not know what I had until now. But even then, the haunting of my rings, tucked away on the glass shelf, still does not leave me alone. I always want to get rid of them, and people around me keep asking why I still live without rings.

I know, I don't know you well. Is it always possible to know a person from two or three whispered conversations when we meet in the library?! But in those conversations, I felt a relief or release from the heavy burden weighing on my soul.

– Why do you sit in the library on Saturdays? I thought you would go home at the end of the week like the other students.

– I'm back, I'm fine with that. I feel free here.

– From housework?

– Of course not.

– Then from what?

– From the rings.

– What rings?

– I don't think I can explain.

– I think I understand you, – you say, remaining silent for a while.

– Then tell me, how can I be freed from those chains?

– You will not be free, you should think that you can fly with them.

– I don't want to.

– Then how long are you going to run away? Maybe you will change your mind when you can truly see someone as your soulmate.

Suddenly, you take my earphones lying on the book and put them to your ears, the words of the song begin to float over the wires:

You from me

Me from you

Don't separate...

– Have you read the novel "Before and After"?

– No.

– Then I advise you to read that book.

– I don't like romantic works.

– Who said that it is romantic?!

– It is known from the name that it is about love.

– I don't think so. If it were up to me, I would call the book "Asymptote".

– Strange. How many works of art can be named after a scientific term?

– If you better understand the essence of

asymptotic* lines, you will understand it. It's just that people recently understood love as only being in love. But there are such loves in this world, in which you do not see the slightest gratitude, the slightest taste, or even reason. What, do you think that people do not have the love that Anvar said to the nurse in book of "Shaytanat"? In fact, he was one hundred percent right. I don't know how, I approve of his opinion.

– I don't see anything here but self–consolation.

– Actually, that's all. The feeling is not in me, but in the heart. Don't be too quick to claim love as yours. We are just a deposit delivery vehicle. Its sole owner is the Creator. He sends His love to His servants in two ways: to some through a person and to others directly. Unfortunately, people do not know that the second is the greatest happiness...

– Then I'm one of the luckiest, – I say with a laugh.

---

* Asymptotic line - (yun . asymptotos – fit does not come) – curve line point get away when you go curve to the line enough level near will be right line. They are very near will come, but never when does not intersect.

You smile:

– Me too.

And I sigh inside. After that, the conversation will not continue, neither you nor I will dare to move on. I feel that I have to go. I gather my things and get up. Only the two of us will be left in the already empty hall. I turn to you and shake my hand. You also open your wide palm to the motionless air and bury yourself in your book until the mucus falls. It means "goodbye".

I will hand the encyclopedia to the librarian. She takes the book, walks around the shelves and disappears. Then she stands up and voices from inside:

– There are two library ID on the table. Take your own.

I will take the one in my hand. Number 127! Something flashes in my mind. I remember that day three months ago when I was the last one to leave the hall.

Isn't it?! The librarian even then...

I look at the ID in one hand and mine lying on the table. I can't decide which one to get...   ✱✱✱

www.ingramcontent.com/pod-product-compliance
Lightning Source LLC
LaVergne TN
LVHW020447070526
838199LV00063B/4869